U.S. WOMEN'S SOCCER: GO FOR GOLD!

by Heather Alexander

Penguin Young Readers
An Imprint of Penguin Random House

People cheer for the United States women's national soccer team. Red, white, and blue confetti fills the air. New York City is having a big parade.

It is the city's first parade for a *female* sports team!

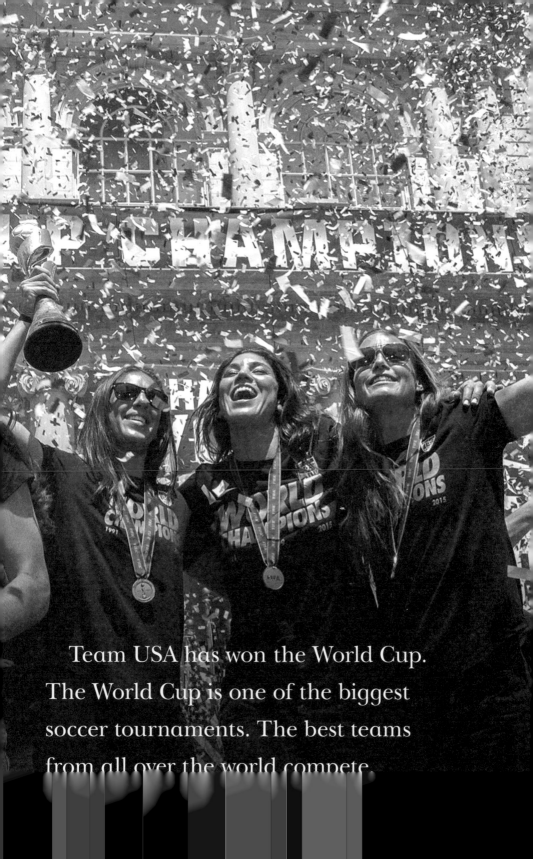

Team USA has won the World Cup. The World Cup is one of the biggest soccer tournaments. The best teams from all over the world compete.

Today, millions of people know the
Team USA players.
But 20 years ago, few people cared
about women's soccer.

Soccer is the most popular sport in the world. It became an Olympic sport for men in 1900. Women's soccer was not added to the Olympics until 1996. That's almost 100 years later! What took so long?

Men thought women could not kick, pass, or head the ball. They thought only men could play soccer.

In the United States, there were no school soccer teams for girls. Girls only played in gym class or on a playground.

In 1972, the US government passed a law. This law said that sports in school had to be equal. If there was a team for boys, there needed to be a team for girls, too.

Women began playing soccer on college teams, high-school teams, and town teams. Any girl could play.

Then, in 1985, the first US women's soccer team was formed.

The first women's World Cup was played in China in 1991. And Team USA won!

There was no parade. The game wasn't shown on TV. Most people did not even know there was a women's soccer team.

Mia Hamm
played for
Team USA in
the first World
Cup. She also
played in the
second World
Cup in 1995.
Team USA came in
third place that year.
But Mia was a star.
She scored 158 goals
in her international
career. That
was the most
goals anyone had
scored—more than
any man or woman!

Women's soccer became an Olympic sport at the 1996 Summer Games. Team USA won the first women's soccer Olympic gold medal!

Most of the Olympic women's soccer games were not shown on TV.

The players wondered: Will people ever care about women's soccer?

Then came the 1999 World Cup.
Team USA played China in the
final. By the end of the game, neither
team had scored. But there had to be a
winner.

Each team was able to take five shots at the goal. The team that got the most shots in would win. Each team got four shots in. US player Brandi Chastain was up last.

Bam! She slammed the ball past China's goalie to win the game for Team USA.

This time the games were shown on TV. Thousands of people watched. They liked women's soccer! All over the country, girls wanted to play on soccer teams, too.

Kristine Lilly takes a shot on goal.

Team USA brought home the silver medal at the Olympic Games in 2000. Norway beat them, but only by one goal. The score was 3–2.

In the 2003 World Cup, Team USA came in third place.

People wondered why they had not won. Had they become worse players?

Not at all! The rest of the world was catching up. Team USA would have to work harder to be number one.

At the 2004 Olympics final, Team USA was tied 1–1 with Brazil. Then, off a corner kick, forward Abby Wambach headed the ball into the goal!

Team USA won the gold.

Over the next few years, Team USA won some big games. They lost some big games, too.

In the 2011 World Cup, Team USA was losing 2–1 in a game against Brazil. There was less than two minutes left. If Team USA did not score soon, they would be out of the World Cup.

The players knew they could not give up. They had to chase down every ball. They had to help one another.

Team USA stole the ball from Brazil. They quickly passed it up the field. From the left side, Megan Rapinoe kicked the ball toward the goal. Abby Wambach was waiting.

Bam! Abby headed the ball in for the goal that helped them win the game.

US player Shannon Boxx takes a shot on goal.

Japan won the 2011 World Cup, but Team USA brought home the silver medal.

Team USA got the gold at the 2012 Olympics. In the final against Japan, Carli Lloyd scored two goals. Goalie Hope Solo made an amazing save. Soon after, Abby Wambach scored even more goals. She broke Mia Hamm's record!

Then it was time for the 2015
World Cup.

Jill Ellis was the coach of Team USA.

She had to choose the best players for
the team.

How did she choose?

She looked for skills that all top soccer players need.

- ☑ Runs fast
- ☑ Kicks the ball far
- ☑ Stops and settles the ball
- ☑ Passes the ball
- ☑ Throws in the ball
- ☑ Heads the ball
- ☑ Stops goals
- ☑ Scores goals
- ☑ Works as a part of the team

The Team USA players showed off their skills at the World Cup.

Forward Alex Morgan ran fast to the ball.

Defender Julie Johnston kicked the ball far up the field.

Forward Morgan Brian stopped and settled the ball.

Midfielder Tobin Heath passed the ball.

Defender Meghan Klingenberg threw the ball in after it went out of bounds.

Midfielder Megan Rapinoe headed the ball. Players can only touch the ball with their feet, chests, and heads. It is a foul if they use their hands.

Hope Solo was the goalie for the World Cup in 2015. Hope holds the US record for the most "clean sheets." A "clean sheet" is when no goals are scored in a game. She won an award for being the best goalie during the tournament.

Carli Lloyd scored three goals in the first 16 minutes of the final against Japan. Scoring three goals in one game is called a "hat trick." Carli was the first female soccer player to do this in a World Cup match, and she did it faster than any male or female player ever had. She won an award, too.

The players worked hard, and they never stopped working together as a team.

Team USA beat Japan 5–2 to win the 2015 World Cup.

Twenty-six million people watched on TV. It was the most-watched soccer game in US history—for men or women! More people watched women's soccer than the basketball finals or the last game of the World Series!

Then it was time for Team USA to get ready for the 2016 Olympics. But they would have to do it without the captain that led them into the World Cup. Abby Wambach retired on December 16, 2015. But Coach Ellis had told her players, "We can't sit still." She said that a team that sits still will get run over. The players had to remember those words now.

They ran sprints. They did push-ups and sit-ups. They did footwork drills.

Coach Ellis had her players practice, practice, practice.

The women of Team USA will never stop trying to be number one.

Now, everyone knows them and cheers for them.

Hopefully there will be many more parades to celebrate Team USA!

Team USA even got to visit the White House where President Barack Obama explained why their win was so important.

"Playing like a girl means being the best," President Obama said. "That's what American women do. That's what American girls do. That's why we celebrate this team."